FRESH BRATS

FRESH
BRATS

X. J. KENNEDY

illustrations by James Watts

Margaret K. McElderry Books
NEW YORK

For all my friends in the Bedford schools,
who aren't brats and never will be

X. J. K.

To my father

J. W.

Text copyright © 1990 by X. J. Kennedy
Illustrations copyright © 1990 by James Watts

Margaret K. McElderry Books
Macmillan Publishing Company
866 Third Avenue
New York, New York 10022
Collier Macmillan Canada, Inc.

First Edition
Printed in the United States of America
10 9 8 7 6 5 4 3 2 1

Library of Congress Cataloging-in-Publication Data is available.

Catalog Number 89-38031
ISBN 0-689-50499-3

Some of this material first appeared in Robert Wallace's
anthologies *Light Year '84, Light Year '85, Light Year '86,*
and *Sometime the Cow Kick Your Head: Light Year '88–9*
(Bits Press).

Lil, to cut the rug's pile lower,
Wheeled in Poppa's power mower,
Making of Mom's rare old Persian
An abbreviated version.

In the pet store Roscoe Rice
Let out all the merchandise:
Infants clapped their hands in glee
Watching pups and chimps run free,
Kittens chasing round the streets
After shrieking parakeets—
How the pet store owner raged!
Roscoe's collared now, and caged.

In the sort of paint that glows
Ross dipped baby sister Rose.
Now at night her folks can find her
By her ghostly pea-green hinder.

Blair, to make his mother screech,
Chugalugged a jug of bleach.
Mother, livid, shook with fright—
"Now how will the wash get white?"

On report-card day Spike Sparks
Scores incredibly high marks.
Is Spike smart? Has he a tutor?
Nope—he's cracked the school computer.

Greg has trained a pig that grunts
Greek and Latin, both at once,
And what's more, it plays Monopoly,
But, as pigs do, somewhat sloppily.

Tell me, why so pale and wan,
Flattened and deflated, John?
Are you weary? Is maintaining
Your vampire bat a wee bit draining?

In the antique glass shop, Knute
Plays a shrill note on his flute.
CRASH!—each precious item shatters.

Father faces money matters.

Sheila, into Dad's right shoe,
Squirts a blob of Superglue,
Does the same thing to the left,
Thus discouraging shoe-theft.
Stuck on fast, they're hard to lose—
Still, who'd be in Father's shoes?

Garth, from off the garden wall,
Ate a rosebush roots and all.
Doctors worked on him for hours.
The family requests, "No flowers."

Stealthy Steffan stuck a dead
Mouse in Mother's rising bread.
My, that fresh-baked loaf smelled nice—
Till, that is, you took a slice.

Every time it rained, mean Merl's
Favorite sport was drenching girls:
With big booted feet he'd stamp
On puddles, getting dresses damp,
Till one wet day Winnie Flood
Flung him backside-flat in mud
And asked him as he sat there soaking,
"How do *you* like that sort of joking?"

Since then, Merl's one of those rare fellas
Who politely share umbrellas.
Oh, how he grew in understanding
From that sudden splashdown landing!

Where the sun shone white-hot, Cass
Held a magnifying glass
Till the school began to burn—
Looks as if she'll never learn.

For his mother's mudpack Brent
Substituted fresh cement.
Mom applied it; in a while
Found it hard to crack a smile.

Sneaky Ebenezer Snyder
Feeds growth hormones to a spider.

Soon, from a whaling-net-sized web,
A shaggy giant jumps on Eb

And makes the selfsame sound, I think,
That straws make, draining dry a drink.

At the fireworks show, rash Randall,
Clinging to a Roman candle,
Took off—whoosh!—across the dark.
"That lad," said Dad, "will make his mark."

In her lunchbox Lena packs
Ornamental fruit of wax,
Adds live worms, a special feature
For her apple for the teacher.

Jen said, "Baby, don't you swaller
That John F. Kennedy half-dollar
Off the tray of your high chair
Even though I laid it there.
Oh, you rotten little kid!
Now look what you went and did!"

From the boat, while Uncle Sid
Wrestles with a giant squid
In a cloud of inky slime,
Frank drawls, "Hey, Unk, got the time?"

Round the 4-H baked goods sale
Brent went waving by the tail
A realistic rubber rat
For the folks to boggle at—
"Guess whose kitchen *this* thing's from!"

No one's bought a single crumb.

Mother! Mother! Bless my soul,
Trisha's flopped the goldfish bowl
Upside down, poor fish and all,
Insisting it's a crystal ball
For telling fortunes. She's predicted
I'll soon drop dead, drug-addicted.
She's foreseen for Bertha Bates
Scads and scads of scary fates—

Mom comes running on the double.
Trisha's future holds big trouble.

With wild mushrooms Madge had found
Mother served the round steak ground.
What a feast! Each guest who tasted
Turned toad-green and toppled, wasted.

Abner from an Alpine height
Launched himself in solo flight.
In the normal course of things,
Arms won't work so well as wings.

On his laboratory table
With a tow-truck's jumper cable,
Frankensteinish Franklin starts
Folks made out of old spare parts.

While, unwatched, the soup pot boils
Baleful Bella pours in oils—
Motor, salad, hair, and baby—
Enough to turn your stomach, maybe.
"This soup," says Dad, "tastes slightly greasy,
But, wow, it sure does slip down easy!"

With her one-string ukelele
Mona drives her dad mad daily,
Twanging songs of one sole note—
What's that jammed down Mona's throat?

From zoo keepers' pails Gail steals
Fish intended for the seals,
Gobbles, gloating, "Ah! Fresh sushi!
Ugh—this one's a wee bit squooshy."

Glenda, in an Everglade,
Cried, "What big eggs something's laid!
Guess I'll wait and watch. I'm curious—"

But what hatched out proved most injurious.

Just before the highest hill
Of the roller coaster Will
(Always one to please a crowd)
Stood up on his seat and bowed.

Obeying gravitation's laws,
The car zoomed on without a pause—
So where's poor William?

Clinging still
To a passing pigeon's bill.

On a trip through Yellowstone,
Desmond held his ice-cream cone
Out for grizzly bears to savor.

Desmond's now their favorite flavor.

Drexel on the ballroom floor
Drizzled Vaseline galore.
Now each dancer who advances
Out on it invents new dances.

Nora, playing with Kit Kitten,
Dangles him her mother's knittin',
Lets his claws catch hold and pull
Till he's wrapped in bright red wool.
Just one more of Nora's errors:
Argyle socks need *human* wearers.

Lancelot, the scurvy knave,
Makes—in Mother's microwave—
Mud pies that look mighty tasty.
Try one, won't you?

                       (Don't be hasty.)

Papa, tumbling down the sky,
Tugs his ripcord, has to sigh.
Out blooms—not his parachute
But some silky substitute
Packed just for a laugh by Greer.
All of the sky divers jeer
As he drifts to earth on Mama's
Pink petunia-print pajamas.

To the bottom of his drink
Dad beholds an earthworm sink.
For her bio project, May
Must have used the ice-cube tray.

To the bowl of champagne punch
At Big Sister's bridal brunch
Edith, jealous little heel,
Introduced a moray eel.

Sparkling conversation bubbled
Yet the caterer looked troubled
When a thing long, wet, and sinister
Cracked the pince-nez off the minister.

Mal, to yank his aching molar,
Strung it to a stopped steamroller.
When that huge machine got going,
All of Mal it went off towing.

To sabotage the Yuletide play
Jealous would-be-actor Jay,
Crouching in the prompter's cage,
Rolls steel marbles out on stage.

Shepherds slip and somersault,
Shouting, "Nuts! It's not my fault!"
One crash-lands on Jay. At last
Someone's put him in a cast.

Sheldon with a welding torch
Gave all four school doors a scorch,
Sealed them shut with bands so stout
Even he could not get out.
Why did Sheldon want to weld?
So he couldn't be expelled.

In a glacier Horace Hind
Made a monumental find:
Four knobby brontosaurus knees
Kept fresh on ice for centuries.

While all the hikers looked on, awed,
A whole big lizard briskly thawed.
"Fear not!" assured Professor Peters,
"These brutes are vegetable eaters."

"But *I'm starved!*" said the brontosaurus.
"I'll skip the salad—pass the Horace!"

On the dam, Neil spied a wheel
That seemed to whisper, "Twist me, Neil!"
"Sure, why not?" thought Neil—which urge
Caused six cities to submerge.

Ocean-bathing, Abner Abb
Down a shark's throat made a grab
For a beach ball it had swallowed.
All the rest of Abner followed.

In the dining car, mean Myrt
Slyly made her grapefruit squirt
Nasty blasts of acid rain—
How she terrorized the train!
Till a crusty old conductor,
Wiping juice from one eye, plucked her
Off her seat—now she's the star
Caged beast in the baggage car.